The Music Fairies

For Ruby Kelsh,
with lots of love

Special thanks to
Sue Mongredien

ORCHARD BOOKS
338 Euston Road, London NW1 3BH
Orchard Books Australia
Level 17/207 Kent Street, Sydney, NSW 2000
A Paperback Original

First published in 2008 by Orchard Books.

© 2008 Rainbow Magic Limited.
A HIT Entertainment company. Rainbow Magic
is a trademark of Rainbow Magic Limited.
Reg. U.S. Pat. & Tm. Off. And other countries.

Illustrations © Orchard Books 2008

A CIP catalogue record for this book is available
from the British Library.

ISBN 978 1 40830 030 5

3 5 7 9 10 8 6 4 2

Printed and bound in China by Imago

Orchard Books is a division of Hachette Children's Books,
an Hachette UK company

www.hachette.co.uk

HiT entertainment

Ellie
the Guitar
Fairy

by Daisy Meadows

ORCHARD BOOKS

www.rainbowmagic.co.uk

I'm through with frost, ice and snow.
To the human world I must go!
I'll form a cool, Gobolicious Band.
Magical instruments will lend a hand.

With these instruments I'll go far.
Frosty Jack, a superstar.
I'll steal music's harmony and fun.
Watch out world, I'll be number one!

Contents

Guitar Star!

Rachel Walker smiled across the breakfast table at her best friend, Kirsty Tate. "Yesterday was a really great start to half term, wasn't it?" she said. "I love our holidays together. We always seem to have the best adventures!"

Rachel was staying with Kirsty's family for a whole week over the autumn half term. The two girls had been friends for a long time, and yesterday they had made some new friends – the Music Fairies!

Kirsty nodded. "It was so exciting meeting Poppy the Piano Fairy, and helping her get her Magic Piano back from the goblins. I loved it when–"

She broke off suddenly. "Did you just hear something?" she asked.

The two girls sat in silence for a moment, listening. Nobody, not even their parents, knew about their fairy friends, and they were careful to keep it that way. It was their most special secret. The two of them had been to Fairyland many times now,

helping all sorts of different fairies and
having some very magical adventures.

Kirsty and Rachel could both hear
footsteps approaching – and another
noise too.

"It sounds like bells," Rachel said in
surprise. "Or a tambourine!" Her eyes
lit up as she turned to Kirsty. "Do you
think it's a musical instrument?"

Yesterday the girls had discovered that Jack Frost had taken all seven of the Music Fairies' Magical Musical Instruments so that he and his goblins could form a pop group – Frosty and his Gobolicious Band. Jack Frost was hoping his band would win the National Talent Competition that was being held in Wetherbury at the end of the week, but the fairies couldn't let that happen. If he did win, it wouldn't take long for people to find out he wasn't human. And once the world knew that fairies really existed, all of Kirsty's and Rachel's magical friends would be in danger of being discovered by nosy humans!

Kirsty, Rachel and Poppy had managed to find the Magic Piano yesterday, but there were still six other missing Magical Musical Instruments that had to be tracked down.

"I don't remember there being a Magic Tambourine," Kirsty replied in a low voice, looking puzzled. Then the kitchen door opened, and her face cleared. "Dad – it's you!"

Mr Tate came into the room, shaking a tambourine enthusiastically. "Morning, girls!" he said cheerfully.

He went over to the table, grabbed a piece of toast and waved goodbye with his tambourine as he walked back to the door.

"Are you having a band practice?" Kirsty asked.

Mr Tate grinned. "We certainly are," he said. "Your Uncle John's already out there warming up on the drums, and Dave's just arrived too."

He winked at Rachel. "Your ears are in for a treat, girls!"

Kirsty laughed as he left the room. "I wouldn't call it a treat," she told Rachel. "They're not very good. And now that the fairies' instruments are missing, Dad's band are going to sound even worse than usual!"

The two girls had learned yesterday that the Music Fairies used their Magical Musical Instruments to help make playing music fun, as well as ensuring that music sounded harmonious all around the world. Since the goblins had taken their Magical Instruments, however, music had sounded flat and tuneless everywhere, and had become far less enjoyable to play or hear.

"Your dad's band can't be that bad," Rachel said, getting to her feet. "Let's go and have a listen."

The two girls left the kitchen and went outside to the barn that stood a short distance from the Tates' house. They peeped around the door to see Mr Tate playing an electric keyboard with one hand and shaking a tambourine with the other. Kirsty's Uncle John was pounding on the

drums, and a third man was taking off his jacket, a guitar case propped up next to him.

"What a racket!" Kirsty whispered to Rachel. "We've got to find those other missing instruments. This is one band that really needs help!"

Rachel had to agree.

"I know the fairies always say that we shouldn't go looking for the magic, and that it'll come to us," she replied. "But maybe if we cycle into Wetherbury, we might find another of the Magical Instruments."

"Good idea," Kirsty said. "The bikes are in the barn. Follow me!"

The girls pushed open the heavy barn door, and the band stopped playing as they went inside.

"What do you think?" Mr Tate called to them. "Think we're in with a shout for the National Talent Competition?"

"You never know," Rachel said, with a smile.

"We won't win anything if we can't keep time," Kirsty's uncle grumbled, setting down his drumsticks with a sigh. "Sorry, lads. I don't know what's wrong with me today. I totally lost the rhythm there."

The two girls exchanged glances. They knew why John was struggling – it was all down to the missing Magical Instruments. They had to find the rest of them!

"No worries," Kirsty's dad said. "Let's practise an easier one next. How about...?" He picked up a pile of paper and the men started discussing lyrics and chord changes.

Kirsty went to get the bikes and accidentally bumped into Dave's guitar case. It fell to the ground with a thud, and popped open. "Oh no!" Kirsty cried, bending down.

The men were so engrossed in their discussion that they hadn't even noticed. Kirsty was about to pick up the guitar

when the sound-hole in the middle
started glowing. Rachel bent down
to take a closer look. "Is it broken?"
she whispered anxiously.

But before Kirsty could reply, there
was a faint strumming sound – and
out flew Ellie the Guitar Fairy!

A Goblin in Disguise?

The girls recognised the little fairy from when they'd met all the Music Fairies the day before, and smiled to see her again now. Ellie was wearing a short, electric blue skirt with sequins on the waistband and a funky net underskirt. She also had on a stripy vest top, leggings and baseball boots.

Her dark hair fanned out around her
face as she flew up to the girls.

"Hello, there!" she said cheerfully.

Kirsty glanced over her shoulder to
where her dad and his friends were still
talking. She didn't want them to notice
Ellie's arrival! "Hi," she said in a low
voice. "We'd better get you out of here
before anyone sees you."

"Sure," Ellie agreed. She flicked her wand at the guitar case, which closed itself neatly — and then she fluttered under Rachel's hair.

Kirsty and Rachel walked quickly out of the barn. "I heard some awful music — that's why I came," Ellie explained. "And now that I'm here, I have a strong feeling that my Magic Guitar is somewhere nearby."

"We'll help you look for it," Rachel said at once, gazing around.

"Although even your Magic Guitar might not be enough to make my dad's band sound any better," Kirsty said, grinning. "That was the awful music you heard."

"Oops," Ellie said, with a tinkling laugh. She fluttered off Rachel's shoulder and hovered in midair, her beating wings a blur of shimmering colours. "Let's start looking anyway, shall we? Where might a goblin have hidden my guitar?"

The three friends were just about to start searching in the garden, when a short, stocky man came up the drive. Kirsty gazed at him with interest. He was wearing a cowboy hat, a long leather coat and enormous sunglasses.

Ellie darted behind the girls as the man approached them.

"Where's the band practising?" he asked in a rather squeaky voice. "I'm the lead singer."

Kirsty's heart thumped. The man was very short – could he possibly be a goblin? With his hat and sunglasses it was hard to tell. Kirsty pointed to the barn, too taken aback to speak.

"Are you thinking what I'm thinking?" Rachel hissed as the man moved out of earshot.

Kirsty nodded. "I've never seen him before," she whispered. "He might be a goblin!"

Ellie raised her eyebrows disbelievingly. "No!" she said. "Goblins are green. You two should know that by now!"

Rachel shook her head. "Jack Frost has cast a spell over the goblins to make them blend in with the humans," she told Ellie. "The goblin we saw yesterday was flesh-coloured, not green."

"He still had big goblin ears and feet," Kirsty said, "and a pointy goblin nose. That was how we could tell he wasn't really human."

"Let's take a closer look at this singer then," Ellie said eagerly, and the three of them went back towards the barn.

They could hear the new arrival singing in a loud screechy voice as they drew nearer. "He is *so* bad," Kirsty whispered in horror. She peeped around the barn door, trying to see the singer's feet. Were they huge goblin feet? It was hard to tell with the cowboy boots he was wearing.

Kirsty tried to creep closer for a better look, but was nearly hit by her Uncle John's drumsticks as he played. Then Rachel tripped on the electric cable from the keyboard and stumbled.

The man in the cowboy hat stopped singing and turned towards her, and Rachel gasped nervously. Oh no! Caught spying! If the singer really was a goblin, he'd be suspicious at once!

Making Music

The singer stretched out a hand to help Rachel to her feet, and smiled at her. "Are you OK?" he asked.

Rachel blushed. "Yes, thanks," she said. Her mind was racing: she knew that goblins were usually very rude. Yet this man had just been kind to her. "Sorry," she went on, "I was just looking for a bike helmet."

"Not a problem," the singer said, tipping his hat to her.

With his hat off, Rachel, Kirsty and Ellie all got a good look at the singer's face. He had normal ears and an ordinary nose. He wasn't a goblin at all!

"Here are the helmets," Kirsty said, handing one to Rachel. "And here's a bike you can borrow."

The girls wheeled the bikes out of the barn quickly. "That was my fault," Kirsty said. "I should have guessed the singer wasn't a goblin by the way my dad and the rest of the band all knew him!"

"Never mind," Rachel said. "We–"
Then she stopped. "Hey," she said,
listening. "It actually sounds as if the
band are playing OK now. They seem
to be getting the hang of it."

Ellie nodded. "And that electric guitar
really rocks!" she added.

Kirsty frowned. "But they don't have
an electric guitar," she said. "Dave's
guitar is an old acoustic one,
remember."

They looked at one another. "So where is that guitar music coming from?" Rachel asked, feeling excited.

They listened again. "This way," Ellie decided, pointing ahead. The girls left their bikes propped up and followed the sound round to the back of the barn. They peered round the corner to see a small figure wearing a leather jacket with a bandana on his head, perched on the wall. An electric guitar was slung over his shoulder.

He wasn't green – but there was no
mistaking the size and shape
of his goblin ears! Ellie
clapped her hands in
excitement. "That's my
guitar!" she whispered.
"It's much bigger
than its usual
Fairyland size, but
it's definitely mine."
Ellie darted behind
Rachel's back as
the goblin finished
playing with a
flourish, then looked up.
He saw the girls watching
him and bowed his head. "I'd
love to stay longer but I've got
places to go," he said grandly.

"Oh that's a shame," Rachel said. "Can't you play some more?" She didn't want the goblin to disappear before they'd thought of a way to get Ellie's guitar back. "I was really enjoying listening to that. You're such a great player."

The goblin smiled, flattered by all the praise. "Well," he said, "perhaps I could stay a little longer..."

"Well done, Rachel," Ellie whispered from her hiding place.

The goblin bent over the guitar and began to play. Seeing him picking out the notes gave Kirsty an idea. "Would you mind showing me a few chords?" she asked him. "I've always wanted to learn to play the guitar and you are the best player I've ever heard."

The goblin looked smug at her comment. "It's true," he agreed. "I *am* the best player in the world. I'm the lead guitarist for Frosty and his Gobolicious Band, you know. Remember that name," he told them. "You're going to be hearing a lot more about our band very soon."

Kirsty went and sat next to him on the wall and watched as he demonstrated a few chords. He couldn't resist showing off with some fancy fingerwork, making the guitar's music ring out in the cool morning air.

"Wow," Kirsty said. "Can I have a go now?" She reached out a hand to take the guitar, planning to snatch it and give it straight to Ellie – but the goblin yanked the guitar away from her. "Nobody but me touches this," he said sternly.

Rachel could hear Ellie giving a cross little tut from behind her. And then it seemed that the indignant fairy wasn't able to keep silent anymore – for suddenly she soared out from her hiding place and hovered in front of the goblin, her hands on her hips. "It's not yours, it's mine," she said hotly. "And I want it back – now!"

A Goblin Trap

Ellie flew straight for the guitar, her fingers stretching out for one of the tuning pegs. The goblin batted her away with the guitar, though, and Ellie had to dodge it quickly to avoid being hit.

Then the goblin backed away from the girls. "I'm going," he said, "and don't waste my time by trying to trick me anymore. I'm off to the Wetherbury Music Shop. Bye!"

"Wait!" Kirsty called out, desperate
for him to stay. "The Wetherbury
Music Shop? Why are you going
there?" she asked.

The goblin had already stormed off
a short way, but he didn't seem able to
resist turning round again. "Because the
so-called best guitarist in the human
world – Wiggy Isapop – is signing his
latest CD there today. But now that
I'm the best guitarist in Fairyland *and*
the human world, I'm going along to
show Wiggy a thing or two."

He turned on his heel and started off again.

"Hold on," Rachel shouted out. "You can't just go into town. You're a goblin! You'll be recognised!"

The goblin put his nose in the air. "Silly girl," he sniffed. "Thanks to Jack Frost's brilliant spell, I look like a human now. No one will ever suspect *me* of being a goblin!"

The girls exchanged glances. The goblin might not be green anymore, but he still didn't look entirely human.

The goblin dashed past them to the barn, where he grabbed Kirsty's bike. He slung the guitar around his back, jumped on the bike and pedalled off.

"Hey! Come back with that!" Kirsty shouted after him, but it was too late. He'd already vanished into the distance.

Rachel sighed in frustration. "Now we've only got one bike between us," she said.

"You cycle, I'll run," Kirsty suggested to her.

Ellie shook her head. "I've got a better idea," she said, and waved her wand over them both. Bright blue fairy dust spiralled out from the tip of her

wand…and the girls immediately
shrank down to fairy size, with delicate
wings appearing on their backs.

Kirsty beamed and zoomed up into
the air. Oh, she did love being a fairy!
"Now we can all fly after the goblin,"
she said. "Good
thinking, Ellie!"

The three fairies
set off towards
Wetherbury.
Kirsty showed
them a short
cut over the fields
so that the goblin
wouldn't see them
following him, and it
only took a few minutes for
them to reach the music shop in town.

They perched on the shop sign and gazed around for the goblin – but couldn't see him.

"I think we've beaten him here," Ellie said. "That gives us some thinking time in which to come up with a plan to get my guitar back."

Rachel fluttered to look around the side of the shop. "There's an alley down here," she told the others. "A dead-end.

It would be good if we could trap the
goblin there somehow."

"How could we lure him into it?"
Kirsty wondered, coming to see.
"Perhaps we
could make some
kind of sign that
would tempt him
down there?"

"Yes," said
Rachel. "And then,
once we've got him trapped, we'll have
a better chance of getting the Magic
Guitar back for you, Ellie."

"And my bike!" Kirsty added.

"Great," Ellie said, brightening at the
thought. "I'd better turn you back into
girls," she decided, and waved her
wand over them.

Glittering blue fairy dust floated all around them, and Kirsty and Rachel felt themselves getting bigger again.

"And maybe we could use something like this, too?" Ellie went on, and waved her wand a second time. Kirsty and Rachel watched in delight as a sparkling, flashing sign appeared on the side of the music shop, with an arrow pointing down the alley. It read, "Lead Guitarists This Way!"

LEAD GUITARISTS
THIS WAY!

Kirsty chuckled. "Perfect," she said. "He won't be able to resist!"

"And just in time, too," Rachel added, seeing a familiar figure coming up the High Street. "Here he comes – hide!"

Splat!

Kirsty and Rachel darted behind a
rubbish bin, with Ellie flying behind
them. "Ugh, it stinks," Kirsty hissed,
fanning a hand in front of her face.
"I think this must be the back of the
greengrocer's — look at all those crates
of old fruit."

The girls and Ellie could see oranges with blue mould on their sides, squishy bruised apples and shrivelled grapes piled up in boxes. "Yuck," Rachel commented. "No wonder they've been thrown out."

"Here comes the goblin," whispered Ellie, peeking around the side of the bin. The girls peered out too and saw him getting off Kirsty's bike and reading the neon sign. "'Lead Guitarists This Way?'" he said to himself in a pleased sort of voice. "That's me!"

He pushed the bike between two
bollards at the end of the alley. He
wasn't really looking where he was
going and walked
straight into a wheelie
bin. An alley cat,
which had been
searching for
food in the bin,
meowed in
fright and leapt
out, claws
outstretched.
The goblin
screamed and
jumped back,
startled, causing
the bike to clatter
to the ground.

Kirsty watched as he struggled to get the bike upright again. She was trying to think of a way for them to get the guitar back, but it was hard to concentrate with the strong smell of rotten fruit. Fruit… Ahh. Maybe they could use the fruit!

"Ellie," she whispered, "if you could fly behind the goblin, he might run further into the alley away from you. Then Rachel and I can pelt him with this rotten fruit!"

Rachel spluttered with giggles and  had to clap a hand over her mouth to keep quiet. Ellie's eyes were bright with mischief. "I love it," the little fairy said.

"Get ready, girls. I'll send him down!"

Ellie zoomed to the end of the alley, high up in the air so the goblin wouldn't notice. Luckily, he was still righting the bike, so he didn't spot her. Then Ellie hovered behind him. "Right," she yelled. "Now I can get my guitar back!"

The goblin jumped when he heard her and swung round.

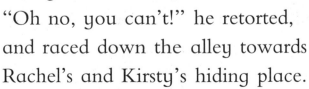

"Oh no, you can't!" he retorted, and raced down the alley towards Rachel's and Kirsty's hiding place.

The plan was working! Both girls
grabbed armfuls of the fruit
from a nearby crate and
began hurling it at the
goblin. Wheeee!
There went a
mouldy grapefruit!
There went a
handful of
soggy plums!

"Aaargh!" the
goblin cried in
alarm, ducking to
avoid the grapefruit.
He wasn't so lucky
with the plums, though –
they splattered over his hair
and the juice ran down his face.
"Not you girls again!" he raged, trying

to wipe it out of his eyes. He took his guitar off his back and held it high, so that none of the fruit would hit it. "You're not getting my guitar so easily," he told them. The goblin glanced behind him, back the way he'd come, and Rachel knew he was thinking about escaping. Her gaze fell upon a box of over-ripe bananas and she knew just what to do. "Ellie! Could you use your magic to scatter these around his feet?" she hissed.

Ellie grinned from where she was floating in midair, and waved her wand. "No problem!" With a stream of sparkling blue fairy dust, the bananas whizzed out of the box and arranged themselves on the ground around the goblin.

Kirsty guessed what her friend's plan was and grabbed some huge watermelons. She rolled them straight towards the goblin like big green bowling balls.

The goblin jumped high over one of the melons…but landed on a slippery banana that squelched under his foot and made him skid. "Whooaaaa!" cried the goblin. He tumbled over, letting go of Ellie's Magic Guitar and sending it flying through the air…

Catch That Guitar!

The girls raced out from their hiding place, dodging all the bananas, hoping to catch the guitar. The goblin, meanwhile, had fallen with a squelch onto a pile of fruit, and was slithering about in it as he tried to get up.

Ellie flung a handful of fairy dust at the guitar as it fell. The blue dust sparkled like glitter in the sunshine, tumbling all around the guitar. There was a puff of blue smoke – and then the guitar shrank to its Fairyland size, and floated down gently.

Rachel stretched up and caught it neatly before it fell to the ground.

"Got it!" she cheered.

The goblin scrambled to his feet, slipping and sliding on the squashed bananas, and howled with rage. "Give that back!" he yelled, lunging for Rachel.

Before the goblin could reach her, though, Ellie had swooped down, and Rachel was able to pass the Magic Guitar up to the little fairy.

"Thank you!" Ellie cried in delight, and soared up high with the guitar, plucking the strings lovingly. "Oh, it's so good to have this back again!"

The goblin glared at her, and jumped up and down, trying to snatch the guitar. "I want that back," he wailed. "How can I be lead guitarist without my guitar?"

Ellie looked down at him. "You know, these Magical Musical Instruments are supposed to help *everyone* enjoy music," she told him.

"I need to take this guitar back to Fairyland where it belongs. But there's nothing to stop you getting your own guitar to play – it would still be fun!"

The goblin stamped his foot. "But I want to be better than Wiggy Isapop," he grumbled.

"Then you need to practise," Ellie told him. "And I need to do some cleaning up here," she went on, gazing around the alley. She played a funky little tune on her Magic Guitar and sang:

"All you fruits down in the street,
put yourselves back,
to make things neat!"

There was a flash of blue light in the alley, and then all the scattered fruit sailed up into the air and returned to the crates.

The sign at the start of the alley
reading "Lead Guitarists This Way" also
disappeared in a cloud of blue glitter.

"There," Ellie smiled. "That's better.
Now the only thing making this place
look messy is *you*," she said to the
goblin. "I think you'd better go back
to Fairyland, don't you?"

The goblin took off his bandana,
wiped the plum juice from his hair,
and then walked away in defeat.

"Wow," Rachel said, looking around at the alley. It looked exactly as it had done when they'd arrived — no one would ever be able to tell there had been a fruit-fight with a goblin just a few moments earlier. "I wish I knew a song like that to tidy my bedroom!"

Ellie chuckled. "Girls, you did a great job helping me get my guitar back," she said to them, flying down to kiss them each on the cheek. Her wings tickled against Rachel's face.

"It was fun," Rachel said. "Especially getting to throw rotten fruit at that goblin!"

"I guess we should go home now," Kirsty said, "and see if Dad's band are any better, now that you've got your guitar back."

Ellie smiled. "I'll return to Fairyland just as soon as I've magicked you home," she said. "I hope you'll hear an improvement in their music. Goodbye!"

She waved her wand in a complicated pattern, and streams of glittery fairy dust whooshed from its tip, all around the girls. Everything blurred before their eyes, and they felt themselves whisked up from the ground in a sparkly whirlwind, with the faint sound of Ellie's funky guitar in their ears. Then they felt themselves land again, and opened their eyes.

They were outside the barn at Kirsty's house, and the bike that the goblin had borrowed was safely back with them too. They could just hear the sound of Mr Tate's band – and to their great surprise, they seemed to be playing in tune now, with a solid drum beat keeping perfect time!

"Ellie's guitar really is amazing," Kirsty said, listening. "They actually sound quite good!"

Rachel grinned. "Maybe they should enter the National Talent Competition after all," she joked.

Kirsty nodded. "First, we've got to stop Jack Frost from winning it with his band," she reminded her friend. "There are five Magical Musical Instruments left to find – and just five days before the competition."

"It's going to be a busy week,"
Rachel said. "And a very musical one
too, I hope!"

Now Rachel and Kirsty must help

Fiona the Flute Fairy

Fiona's Magic Flute is missing and she
needs Rachel's and Kirsty's help to
outwit the naughty goblins and
get it back...

Here's an extract from
Fiona the Flute Fairy...

Card Trick

"Oh, this is one of my favourite shops in Wetherbury!" Rachel Walker stopped outside *Sparkly Wishes* and turned to her best friend, Kirsty Tate. "They always have such gorgeous cards and gifts. Can we go in?"

"OK," Kirsty agreed, pushing open the shop door. "Do you want to buy something or just look around?"

"I want to get a thank you card to give to your parents when I go home at the end of half term," Rachel replied, as they went inside.

Kirsty smiled. "Oh, that's lovely!"

"I'll get a card to send to Mum and Dad, too," Rachel went on, "Just to say that I'm fine, and having a great time." She grinned. "Although Mum and Dad know that I always have a great time when I stay with you, Kirsty."

"They don't know that we're friends with the fairies and have lots of exciting, magical adventures, though!" Kirsty pointed out.

Rachel nodded. The Music Fairies had asked for the girls' help after Jack Frost and his naughty goblin servants had stolen the seven Magical Musical Instruments from the Fairyland School of Music. These special instruments made music fun and harmonious in both the human and fairy worlds,

and without them, music everywhere
sounded terrible and out of tune.

Rachel and Kirsty had been horrified
to discover that Jack Frost intended to
use the instruments' magical powers
to win the National Talent Competition
that was taking place at the New
Harmony Mall near Wetherbury.
Jack Frost was determined to win the
first prize of a recording contract with
MegaBig Records, and had sent his
goblins to hide out in Wetherbury with
the Magical Musical Instruments, ready
for the competition at the weekend.
But, with the help of the Music Fairies,
the girls were determined to foil his
plans and return all the instruments to
Fairyland before Rachel went home
at the end of half term.

"I hope we find another Magical Musical Instrument today," Rachel said, as she flipped through a rack of glittery cards. "We've managed to return Poppy's piano and Ellie's guitar, but we need to find all the other instruments, so music isn't ruined forever!"

"I know," Kirsty agreed. "But remember what Queen Titania always says? We have to let the magic come to *us*."

"It's hard though, isn't it?" Rachel sighed.

"*Really* hard!" Kirsty nodded...

Win Rainbow Magic goodies!

In every book in the Rainbow Magic Music Fairies series (books 64-70) there is a hidden picture of a musical note with a secret letter in it. Find all seven letters and re-arrange them to make a special Music Fairies word, then send it to us. Each month we will put the entries into a draw and select one winner to receive a Rainbow Magic Sparkly T-shirt and Goody Bag!

Send your entry on a postcard to Rainbow Magic Music Fairies Competition, Orchard Books, 338 Euston Road, London NW1 3BH. Australian readers should write to Hachette Children's Books, Level 17/207 Kent Street, Sydney, NSW 2000. New Zealand readers should write to Rainbow Magic Competition, 4 Whetu Place, Mairangi Bay, Auckland, NZ. Don't forget to include your name and address. Only one entry per child. Final draw: 30th September 2009.

Good luck!

Have you checked out the

website at:

www.rainbowmagic.co.uk

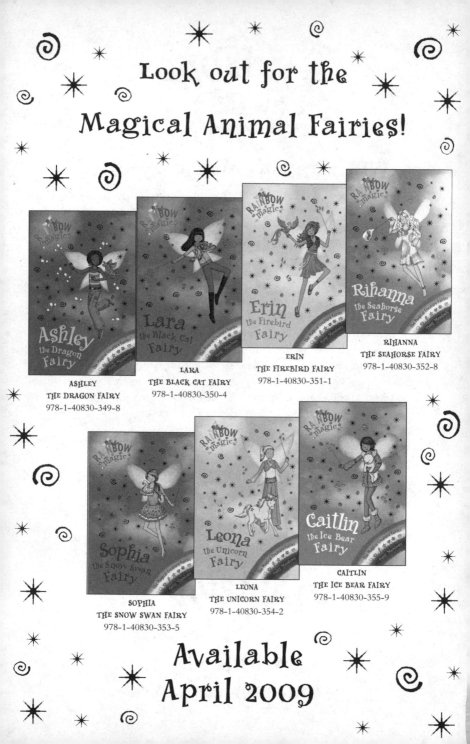

Look out for the
Magical Animal Fairies!

ASHLEY
THE DRAGON FAIRY
978-1-40830-349-8

LARA
THE BLACK CAT FAIRY
978-1-40830-350-4

ERIN
THE FIREBIRD FAIRY
978-1-40830-351-1

RIHANNA
THE SEAHORSE FAIRY
978-1-40830-352-8

SOPHIA
THE SNOW SWAN FAIRY
978-1-40830-353-5

LEONA
THE UNICORN FAIRY
978-1-40830-354-2

CAITLIN
THE ICE BEAR FAIRY
978-1-40830-355-9

Available
April 2009